Susan Jeffers

Hansel & Gretel

by *The Brothers Grimm* ✦ *retold by Amy Ehrlich*

DUTTON CHILDREN'S BOOKS
An Imprint of PENGUIN GROUP (USA) INC.

DUTTON CHILDREN'S BOOKS
A division of Penguin Young Readers Group

Published by the Penguin Group
Penguin Group (USA) Inc., 375 Hudson Street, New York, New York 10014, U.S.A.
Penguin Group (Canada), 90 Eglinton Avenue East, Suite 700, Toronto, Ontario, Canada M4P 2Y3 (a division of Pearson Penguin Canada Inc.)
Penguin Books Ltd, 80 Strand, London WC2R 0RL, England
Penguin Ireland, 25 St Stephen's Green, Dublin 2, Ireland (a division of Penguin Books Ltd)
Penguin Group (Australia), 250 Camberwell Road, Camberwell, Victoria 3124, Australia (a division of Pearson Australia Group Pty Ltd)
Penguin Books India Pvt Ltd, 11 Community Centre, Panchsheel Park, New Delhi - 110 017, India
Penguin Group (NZ), 67 Apollo Drive, Rosedale, Auckland 0632, New Zealand (a division of Pearson New Zealand Ltd)
Penguin Books (South Africa) (Pty) Ltd, 24 Sturdee Avenue, Rosebank, Johannesburg 2196, South Africa
Penguin Books Ltd, Registered Offices: 80 Strand, London WC2R 0RL, England

CIP Data is available.

Published in the United States by Dutton Children's Books,
a division of Penguin Young Readers Group
345 Hudson Street, New York, New York 10014
www.penguin.com/youngreaders

Originally published in 1980 by Dial Books for Young Readers

The full-color artwork was prepared using a fine-line pen with ink and dyes.
They were applied over a detailed pencil drawing that was then erased.

A Note on the Text
This translation of *Hänsel and Gretel* was originally included in a collection entitled
Fairy Tales of the Brothers Grimm by Mrs. Edgar Lucas,
published in 1902 by J.B. Lippincott Company.
The language has been altered only as necessary to avoid archaic references.

Designed by Beth Herzog
Manufactured in China

Revised Edition

ISBN 978-0-525-42221-1
1 3 5 7 9 10 8 6 4 2

For Dad, Caroline, and Bill

At the edge of a large forest there once lived a poor woodcutter with his wife and two children, Hansel and Gretel. A terrible famine came to the land, and the woodcutter could not even provide food for his family.

One night he lay awake, worrying. "What is to become of us?" he said
to his wife. "How can we feed our poor children when we have nothing?"

"I'll tell you what," she answered. "Tomorrow we will take the children
out into the forest and leave them there. They won't be able to find their way
home, and so we shall be rid of them."

"No, I could never leave my children alone in the forest," said the woodcutter. "The wild animals would soon tear them to pieces."

"What a fool!" the woman said. "Then we must all die of hunger." And she gave him no peace until he consented.

But the two children had not been able to sleep, and they heard what their stepmother had said.

Gretel wept bitterly. "All is over for us now."

"Don't cry, Gretel," said Hansel. "I'll find a way to save us."

When the woodcutter and his wife were asleep, Hansel slipped out the door. The moon was shining brightly, and the white pebbles around the house gleamed like silver coins. Hansel stooped down and gathered as many pebbles as his pockets would hold.

Then he went back to Gretel. "Go to sleep now," he said. "We will not perish in the forest."

At daybreak, the woman came to wake them. "Get up, you lazybones," she ordered. "We are going to fetch wood." She gave them each a piece of bread. "Here is something for your dinner, but do not eat it right away, for it's all you get."

When they had gone a little way into the forest, Hansel stopped to look back at the cottage, and he did it again and again.

"What are you doing?" his father asked. "Keep up with us."

"Oh, Father," said Hansel. "It's my white cat. It is sitting on the roof, saying good-bye to me."

"Little fool!" the woman said. "That is no cat. It's the morning sun shining on the chimney."

But Hansel had not been looking at the cat at all. Each time he stopped, he had dropped a white pebble on the ground to mark the way.

Once in the forest, their father made a fire to warm them. The woman said, "Now rest here while we go cut wood. We will come back later to fetch you."

Hansel and Gretel sat by the fire, and soon they fell fast asleep.

When they awoke, it was dark night. Gretel began to cry. "How shall we ever get out of the forest?"

But Hansel comforted her. "When the moon rises, we will find our way."

Hansel took his sister by the hand, and they began to walk, guided by the pebbles that glittered like bits of silver in the moonlight.

At daybreak they finally reached their father's cottage.

"You bad children!" said the woman when she saw them. "Why did you sleep for so long in the forest?"

But their father was glad, for it had hurt him sorely to leave them behind.

Later, Hansel and Gretel heard the woman talking. "Soon we will have nothing to eat. The children must go away. There is nothing else to be done."

The woodcutter tried to protest, but it was to no use.

When everything was quiet, Hansel tried to go out for more pebbles, but the woman had locked the door.

In the early morning the woman made the children get up, gave them each a very small bit of bread, and led them into the forest. As they walked Hansel dropped bread crumbs on the ground.

The woman brought the children to a place where they had never been before.

"Stay here, children," she said. "And when you are tired, you may go to sleep. We are going to cut wood, and in the evening we will come back and fetch you."

At dinnertime Gretel shared her bread with Hansel.
They went to sleep, and the evening passed, but no one
came to fetch them.

It was dark when they woke up. Hansel comforted
his sister and held her close. "Wait until the moon rises,"
he said. "Then we can see the bread crumbs that I scattered
for a path."

As the moon rose, they started out but they found no bread crumbs.
They did not know that birds who lived in the forest had eaten every one.

They walked all night and the next morning, but they could not get out of the forest.

They were very hungry, and they began to fear that if no help came they would perish.

Then, at midday, they saw a beautiful snow-white bird. Hansel and Gretel followed it until they came to a little house, wonderful beyond their dreams.

The house was made entirely of cake, and it was roofed with icing. The windows were transparent sugar. The children were so hungry that they did not hesitate at all. Hansel stretched up and broke off a piece of the roof, and Gretel went to the window and began to nibble at that. Then a gentle voice called out to them:

"Nibbling, nibbling like a mouse,
Who's that nibbling at my house?"

All at once the door opened and an old, old woman hobbled out. Hansel and Gretel were so frightened that the food they were eating fell from their hands.

"Ah, dear children," the old woman said. "Come in and stay with me."

She took them by their hands and led them into the little house. A fine dinner was set before them.

After they had eaten, she took them to two small beds. When Hansel and Gretel fell asleep, they felt as if they were in heaven.

But the old woman was really a witch. She had built the cake house especially to lure children to her.

Witches have red eyes and can't see very far, but their sense of smell is as keen as an animal's, and they know when human beings come close. The witch liked children best of all. Whenever she snared one, she cooked it and ate it and considered it a grand feast.

24

When Hansel and Gretel were asleep, she laughed wickedly. "Now I have them," she said. "They shan't escape me."

Early in the morning, she shut Hansel up in a little stable and barred the door. Though he shrieked at the top of his lungs, she took no notice of him.

Then she shook Gretel awake. "Get up, you lazybones. Fetch some water and cook something for your brother. When he is nice and fat, I will eat him."

Gretel began to cry bitterly, but she had to obey the witch's orders.

Every morning the old witch hobbled to the stable and ordered Hansel to hold out his finger so she could feel how fat he was.

But Hansel held out a bone instead. The witch's eyes were dim, and she thought the bone was Hansel's finger and wondered why he did not get any fatter.

When four weeks had passed, she would wait no longer. "Now then, Gretel," she said. "Fetch the water. Fat or thin, I will kill Hansel and eat him."

How Gretel grieved! As she carried the water the tears streamed down her cheeks.

"We will bake first," said the witch. "I have heated the oven and kneaded the dough. Creep in and see if the fire is blazing high enough now." And she pushed Gretel toward the oven.

The witch meant to shut the door and roast her once she was inside. But Gretel saw what she had in mind. "I don't know how to get in," she said. "How am I to manage it?"

"Stupid goose!" said the witch, rushing up to the oven. "The opening is big enough. See, I could fit myself."

Quickly, Gretel gave the witch a push, then she banged the door and bolted it tight.

The witch howled horribly.

Gretel ran to the stable as fast as she could and opened the door.

"Hansel! Hansel!" she cried. "We are saved. The old witch is dead!"

Hansel rushed out like a bird from a cage when the door was opened. They danced around with joy.

In the witch's house they found chests full of pearls and precious jewels. Hansel filled his pockets and Gretel filled her apron, and then they hurried away.

As they walked through the forest, the trees and hills became more and more familiar to them. At last they saw their father's house in the distance.

Hansel and Gretel rushed inside and threw their arms around their father's neck. The poor man had not had a single moment of peace or pleasure since he had deserted his children in the forest, and while they were gone, his wife had died.

Gretel scattered the pearls and jewels all over the floor. Hansel added handful after handful out of his pockets.

From that time all their troubles were ended, and they lived together in great happiness.